Geronimo Stilton

ENGLISH!

4 HOW OLD ARE YOU? 你幾歲了？

U0061303

新雅文化事業有限公司
www.sunya.com.hk

Geronimo Stilton English
HOW OLD ARE YOU? 你幾歲了？

作　　者：Geronimo Stilton 謝利連摩·史提頓
譯　　者：申倩
責任編輯：王燕參
封面繪圖：Giuseppe Facciotto
插圖繪畫：Claudio Cernuschi, Andrea Denegri, Daria Cerchi
內文設計：Angela Ficarelli, Raffaella Picozzi
出　　版：新雅文化事業有限公司
　　　　　香港筲箕灣耀興道3號東匯廣場9樓
　　　　　營銷部電話：（852）2562 0161
　　　　　客戶服務部電話：（852）2976 6559
　　　　　傳真：（852）2597 4003
　　　　　網址：http://www.sunya.com.hk
　　　　　電郵：marketing@sunya.com.hk
發　　行：香港聯合書刊物流有限公司
　　　　　香港新界大埔汀麗路36號中華商務印刷大廈3字樓
　　　　　電話：（852）2150 2100　傳真：（852）2407 3062
　　　　　電郵：info@suplogistics.com.hk
印　　刷：C & C Offset Printing Co.,Ltd
　　　　　香港新界大埔汀麗路36號
版　　次：二〇一一年二月初版
　　　　　10 9 8 7 6 5 4 3 2 1

CONTENTS
目 錄

BENJAMIN'S CLASSMATES
班哲文的老師和同學們

Maestra Topitilla
托比蒂拉·德·托比莉斯

Rarin
拉琳

Diego
迪哥

Rupa
露芭

Tui
杜爾

David
大衛

Sakura
櫻花

Mohamed
穆哈麥德

Tian Kai
田凱

Oliver
奧利佛

Milenko
米蘭哥

Trippo
特里普

Carmen
卡敏

Atina
阿提娜

Esmeralda
愛絲梅拉達

Pandora
潘朵拉

Takeshi
北野

Kuti
菊花

Benjamin
班哲文

Hsing
阿星

Laura
羅拉

Kiku
奇哥

Antonia
安東妮婭

Liza
麗莎

GERONIMO AND HIS FRIENDS
謝利連摩和他的家鼠朋友們

謝利連摩・史提頓 Geronimo Stilton
一個古怪的傢伙，簡直可以說是一隻笨拙的文化鼠。他是《鼠民公報》的總裁，正花盡心思改變報紙業的歷史。

菲・史提頓 Tea Stilton
謝利連摩的妹妹，她是《鼠民公報》的特派記者，同時也是一個運動愛好者。

班哲文・史提頓 Benjamin Stilton
謝利連摩的小姪兒，常被叔叔稱作「我的小乳酪」，是一隻感情豐富的小老鼠。

潘朵拉・華之鼠 Pandora Woz
柏蒂・活力鼠的小姪女、班哲文最好的朋友，是一隻活潑開朗的小老鼠。

柏蒂・活力鼠 Patty Spring
美麗迷人的電視新聞工作者，致力於她熱愛的電視事業。

賴皮 Trappola
謝利連摩的表弟，非常喜歡食物，風趣幽默，是一隻饞嘴、愛開玩笑的老鼠，善於將歡樂傳遞給每一隻鼠。

麗萍姑媽 Zia Lippa
謝利連摩的姑媽，對鼠十分友善，又和藹可親，只想將最好的給身邊的鼠。

艾拿 Iena
謝利連摩的好朋友，充滿活力，熱愛各項運動，他希望能把對運動的熱誠傳給謝利連摩。

史奎克・愛管閒事鼠 Ficcanaso Squitt
謝利連摩的好朋友，是一個非常有頭腦的私家偵探，總是穿着一件黃色的乾濕褸。

HAPPY BIRTHDAY, BENJAMIN!
班哲文，生日快樂！

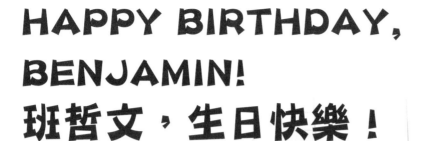

親愛的小朋友，今天是一個特別的日子——班哲文的生日！我打算為我的「小乳酪」舉辦一個生日派對，你願意幫助我嗎？他的朋友們都會來參加，生日派對中會有生日蛋糕、很多禮物和各種美味得讓你鬍子翹起來的茶點！現在就跟班哲文和他的朋友們一起來唱歌跳舞吧，你還可以學到怎樣用英語說祝賀生日的話，以及如何向別人詢問年齡和說出自己喜歡和不喜歡吃的茶點呢。來吧，班哲文馬上就到了，讓我們給他一個驚喜吧！

> It's Benjamin's birthday today!

happy	快樂
birthday	生日
party	派對
very	很

Let's prepare the party!

Benjamin's birthday
班哲文的生日

I'm very happy today!

跟我謝利連摩·史提頓一起學英文，就像玩遊戲一樣簡單好玩！

你可以一邊看着圖畫一邊讀。
以下有幾個標誌，你要特別留意：

🧀 當看到 💿 標誌時，你可以聽CD，一邊聽，一邊跟着朗讀，還可以跟着一起唱歌。

🧀 當看到 ⭐ 標誌時，你可以和朋友們一起玩遊戲，或者嘗試回答問題。題目很簡單，它們對鞏固你所學過的內容很有幫助。

🧀 當看到 ❗ 標誌時，你要注意看一下格子裏的生字，反覆唸幾遍，掌握發音。

最後，不要忘記完成小測驗和練習冊裏的問題！看看你有多聰明吧。

祝大家學得開開心心！

謝利連摩·史提頓

BENJAMIN'S BIRTHDAY PARTY 班哲文的生日派對

潘朵拉和柏蒂正忙着用氣球和彩帶布置謝利連摩家的客廳。賴皮帶來了一些糕點和小食，不過要準備的事情還多着呢。菲正在列寫一個派對所需物品的清單，請跟她一起用英語說出來吧。

table	桌子	plate	碟子	jug	壺
tablecloth	桌布	spoon	匙子	juice	果汁
napkin	餐巾	fork	叉子	ribbon	彩帶
glass	玻璃杯	bottle	瓶子	balloon	氣球

現在我們學習從11數到15！

⭐ 柏蒂共掛了多少個氣球？試着用英語說出來。

11 eleven
12 twelve
13 thirteen
14 fourteen
15 fifteen

答案：fourteen balloons

班哲文一進門，所有鼠都立刻鼓掌，並祝他生日快樂！我對他說今天是他的生日，他馬上跑過來給我一個大大的擁抱。這時候，賴皮用手推車送來了他一早預備好的美味茶點，請跟他一起用英語說出來吧。

biscuits	餅乾
sandwich	三文治
wafer	威化餅
toast	多士
mini-pizza	迷你薄餅
French fries	薯條
sweet	糖果
chips	薯片
lollipop	波板糖
cheese	乳酪
ice cream	雪糕
jelly	啫喱
cherry	車厘子

⭐ 看，賴皮多饞嘴啊，他目不轉睛地盯着面前手推車上的美食！你能用英語說出這些食物的名稱嗎？試試看。

答案：在賴皮面前的手推車上放著：biscuits, wafers, chips, French fries, lollipops, cherries, ice cream, cheese and jelly.

9

LOOK AT ALL THESE PRESENTS! 看！好多禮物啊！

門鈴響了。是誰來了？班哲文立刻跑去開門……哇，真是一個大驚喜，原來是班哲文的好朋友們來了，而且他們還帶來了好多禮物！請你跟着班哲文一起用英語說出他收到了哪些禮物！

present	禮物	address book	地址簿
belt	皮帶	basketball	籃球
T-shirt	T恤	basketball stand	籃球架
cup	杯子	cap	鴨舌帽
book	書	poster	海報

A present for you!

Look at all these presents!

This is for you!

⚫ surprise 驚喜
How lovely! 多可愛啊！

⭐ 潘朵拉送給班哲文什麼禮物？請用英語回答。

Surprise!

What a nice surprise!

How lovely! Thank you!

答案：a basketball stand and a basketball

10

BENJAMIN'S BIRTHDAY CAKE 班哲文的生日蛋糕

瑪嘉蓮姑媽和瑪思卡波姑丈也來了，他們還帶着他們的雙胞胎女兒梵提娜和芳多兒一起來。瑪嘉蓮姑媽帶來了很多好吃的食物和飲品。請你試着跟她用英語說出來吧！

cake	蛋糕
chocolate	朱古力
fruit	水果
apple	蘋果
a box of biscuits	一盒餅乾
birthday cake	生日蛋糕
fruit cake	鮮果蛋糕
apple pie	蘋果批
orange juice	橙汁
lemonade	檸檬水
chocolate cake	朱古力蛋糕
a box of chocolates	一盒朱古力

⭐ 1. 柏蒂手爪上拿着的是什麼？請用英語回答。

⭐ 2. 我感到肚子有點餓了，你知道我伸出手爪想拿什麼嗎？請用英語回答。

⭐ 3. 潘朵拉的小手推車上放的是什麼？請用英語回答。

答案：1. birthday cake   2. biscuits   3. a chocolate cake

11

HAPPY BIRTHDAY!
生日快樂!

柏蒂在蛋糕上插了九枝蠟燭,然後大家一起唱生日歌,你也和大家一起唱生日歌吧!

A SONG FOR YOU! Track 1

Happy Birthday,
Dear Benjamin!

Happy birthday
dear Benjamin,
it's your birthday,
dear Benjamin,
happy birthday
dear Benjamin...
Happy birthday,
happy day!

Blow out the candles!

Blow out the candles!

班哲文吹滅了蠟燭後，大家一起鼓掌慶祝！柏蒂把蛋糕切開，分給客人們吃。不到一會兒，班哲文的碟子已經空了，於是他走去找柏蒂，你知道他想做什麼嗎？看看他們的對話吧。

candle 蠟燭
a piece of cake 一塊蛋糕

Would you like another piece of cake?

Would you like?
你喜歡嗎？
I would like
我喜歡

No, thanks! I would like some orange juice.

⭐ 1. 黃色托盤內還剩下蛋糕多少塊？請用英語回答。

⭐ 2. 紅色托盤內還剩下餅乾多少塊？請用英語回答。

⭐ 3. 綠色托盤內還剩下迷你薄餅多少塊？請用英語回答。

答案：*1. four pieces of cake*   *2. twelve biscuits*   *3. thirteen mini-pizzas*

HOW OLD ARE YOU?
你幾歲了？

賴皮跟班哲文和他的朋友們一起玩，他逐個詢問他們的年紀……但他們的答案卻都一樣，因為他們是同班同學嘛！你也跟着他們一起用英語回答吧！

I AM NINE. 我九歲。

賴皮跟小朋友玩完遊戲後，柏蒂也來湊熱鬧，她想唱一首她非常喜歡的歌給大家聽。班哲文和他的好朋友們都很開心，你也跟着他們一起唱吧！

A SONG FOR YOU! Track 2

I Am Nine

I am nine, I am nine,
I'm so happy, I am nine!
This is my birthday with my friends,
I'm very happy!
You are nine, you are nine,
you're so happy, you are nine!
This is your birthday with your friends,
you're very happy!
Oh, wow, we are so happy...
it's our birthday!
She is nine, she is nine,
she's so happy, she is nine!
This is her birthday with her friends,
she's very happy!
He is nine, he is nine,
he's so happy, he is nine!

This is his birthday with his friends,
he's very happy!
Oh, wow, we are so happy...
it's our birthday!
We are nine, we are nine,
we're so happy, we are nine!
This is our birthday with our friends,
we're very happy!
You are nine, you are nine,
you're so happy, you are nine!
This is your birthday with your friends,
you're very happy!
Oh, wow, we are so happy...
it's our birthday!
They are nine, they are nine,
they're so happy, they are nine!
This is their birthday with their friends,
they're very happy!
Oh, wow, we are so happy...
it's our birthday!

I LIKE FRUIT CAKE!
我喜歡吃鮮果蛋糕！

生日派對上有很多美味的食物，梵提娜和芳多兒最喜歡吃鮮果蛋糕，奧利佛喜歡吃雪糕，阿提娜喜歡吃三文治，迪哥偏愛迷你薄餅……一起來看看班哲文的其他朋友們喜歡吃什麼，試着用英語說出來吧。

Do you like to have another piece of fruit cake?

Me too.

Yes, please! I like fruit cake.

I like sandwiches.

I like mini-pizzas.

I like ice cream.

I like orange juice.

I like pear juice.

I like sweets.

I like biscuits.

! **Yes, please!**
好的，謝謝！

! **I like**
我喜歡
I don't like
我不喜歡

I DON'T LIKE APPLE PIE!
我不喜歡吃蘋果批！

賴皮是一隻饞嘴鼠，無論什麼都愛吃，不過，不過……他卻不喜歡吃蘋果批！現在每隻老鼠都要說出自己不喜歡吃的食物，請你跟他們一起用英語說說看。

I don't like apple pie.

I don't like lemonade.

> ! **sandwich**
> 三文治
> **sandwiches**
> sandwich 的眾數

I don't like toast.

I don't like chips.

I don't like sandwiches.

⭐ 1. 在剛剛學到的那麼多茶點和飲品中，你最喜歡的是什麼？請用英語回答。

I like ...

I don't like honey cakes.

I don't like cherries.

⭐ 2. 現在試着用英語說出你不喜歡吃的食物。

I don't like ...

LET'S PLAY MUSICAL CHAIRS! 一起來玩音樂椅！

生日派對繼續進行着，這時，潘朵拉提議大家來玩一個遊戲——音樂椅遊戲！但不是所有小朋友都知道這個遊戲的玩法，因此柏蒂給小朋友們講述了一遍遊戲規則，請跟着她一起說吧。

1. Everybody, except for Benjamin, takes a chair and puts it in a circle.

2. While the music is playing, Benjamin, Pandora and their friends walk or dance around.

3. Geronimo stops the music and the others try to sit on a chair.

4. The one left without a chair is out and takes a chair away.

5. The game is over when there's only one player left and no chairs!

現在大家都清楚遊戲的規則了，你也和你的朋友一起來玩這個遊戲吧。試着用英語給他們說明遊戲規則。

A SURPRISE PARTY

It's Geronimo Stilton's birthday and his sister Tea is organizing a surprise party for him...

Who's going to bring the birthday cake?

I'll get it.

And I'll get the drinks.

I'll get the plates, trays and napkins.

〈一個驚喜的派對〉

今天是謝利連摩的生日。她的妹妹菲打算為他舉行一個驚喜的派對。

菲：誰會去拿蛋糕？

賴皮：我去拿。

柏蒂：我去拿飲品。

史丹塔：我去拿碟子、托盤和餐巾。

20

當所有人正忙着為派對準備食物和飲品的時候，班哲文和潘朵拉在製作一張生日卡給謝利連摩。

潘朵拉：我們應該寫什麼呢？
班哲文：「祝你生日快樂！」

潘朵拉：好，然後呢？
班哲文：我們畫些圖畫吧。

班哲文：但畫些什麼好呢？

潘朵拉：我有一個好主意！

賴皮：生日蛋糕到了，現在只欠蠟燭。

菲：蠟燭在這裏！快，謝利連摩快要來了……

菲剛把燈關掉，賴皮馬上伸出手爪想偷薯片吃。

菲：賴皮，不要偷吃！

Geronimo Stilton opens the door: all is quiet in the room.

謝利連摩打開大門，屋內靜悄悄的。

It's dark here and there's nobody...what a pity...

謝利連摩：這裏黑漆漆的，一個人也沒有……我真可憐……

...right on my birthday!

謝利連摩：……今天可是我的生日啊！

Happy birthday!

班哲文和潘朵拉：生日快樂！

Thank you, my friends! What an exciting birthday!

The End

謝利連摩：我的朋友們，謝謝大家！這真是一個令人興奮的生日！

23

TEST 小測驗

⭐ 1. 你知道怎麼用英語說出下面的數字嗎？說說看。

11　　**12**　　**13**　　**14**　　**15**

⭐ 2. 用英語說出以下食品的名稱。

雪糕　　迷你薄餅　　糖果　　餅乾　　橙汁　　蜜糖蛋糕　　檸檬水

⭐ 3. 你今年幾歲了？請用英語回答。

I am ...　　　　**I'm ...**

⭐ 4. 你知道怎樣用英語說出下面的詞語嗎？說說看。

禮物　　　　書　　　　T 恤　　　　籃球

⭐ 5. 用英語說出下面的句子。

(a) 我喜歡吃朱古力蛋糕。

I like ...

(b) 我不喜歡吃乳酪。

I don't like ...

(c) 我喜歡吃糖果。

I like ...

(d) 我不喜歡吃迷你薄餅。

I don't like ...

DICTIONARY 詞典

（英、粵、普發聲）

A

a box of biscuits　　一盒餅乾

a box of chocolates

　　一盒朱古力　（普：一盒巧克力）

a piece of cake　　一塊蛋糕

address book　　地址簿

another　　另一個

apple　　蘋果

apple pie　　蘋果批　（普：蘋果派）

B

balloon　　氣球

basketball　　籃球

basketball stand　　籃球架

belt　　皮帶

birthday　　生日

birthday cake　　生日蛋糕

birthday card　　生日卡

biscuits　　餅乾

blow out　　吹滅

book　　書

bottle　　瓶子

busy　　忙碌

C

cake　　蛋糕

candle　　蠟燭

cap　　鴨舌帽

chair　　椅子

cheese　　乳酪

cherry　　車厘子　（普：櫻桃）

chips　　薯片

chocolate　　朱古力　（普：巧克力）

chocolate cake

　　朱古力蛋糕　（普：巧克力蛋糕）

circle　　圓圈

cup　杯子

D

dance　跳舞

dark　黑漆漆的

door　門

draw　畫畫

drinks　飲品

E

eleven　十一

everybody　每個人

except　除了……之外

exciting　令人興奮的

F

fifteen　十五

food　食物

fork　叉子

fourteen　十四

French fries　薯條

friends　朋友

fruit　水果

fruit cake　鮮果蛋糕

G

game　遊戲

glass　玻璃杯

H

happy　快樂

I

ice cream　雪糕

idea　主意

J

jelly　啫喱（普：果凍）

jug　壺

juice　果汁

L

lemonade　檸檬水

light　燈

like　喜歡

lollipop

　　波板糖（普：棒棒糖）

lovely　可愛的

M

me too　我也是

mini-pizza　迷你薄餅

music　音樂

N

napkin　餐巾

nice　好

nine　九

No, thanks!　不，謝謝！

O

opens　打開

orange juice　橙汁

P

party　派對

plate　碟子

poster　海報

prepare　準備

present　禮物

Q

quick　快

quiet　靜悄悄的

R

ribbon　彩帶

room　房間

S

sandwich

　三文治（普：三明治）

spoon　匙子

steal　偷

stop　停止

surprise　驚喜

sweet　糖果

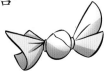

T

table　桌子

tablecloth　桌布

thank you　謝謝

thirteen　十三

toast　多士（普：烤麵包片）

today　今天

tray　托盤

try　嘗試

T-shirt　T恤（普：汗衫）

turn off　關掉

twelve　十二

W

wafer　威化餅

walk　走路

what a pity　真可憐

write　寫

Y

Yes, please!　好的，謝謝！

看在一千塊莫澤雷勒乳酪的份上，你學得開心嗎？很開心，對不對？好極了！跟你一起跳舞唱歌我也很開心！我等着你下次繼續跟班哲文和潘朵拉一起玩一起學英語呀。現在要說再見了，當然是用英語說啦！

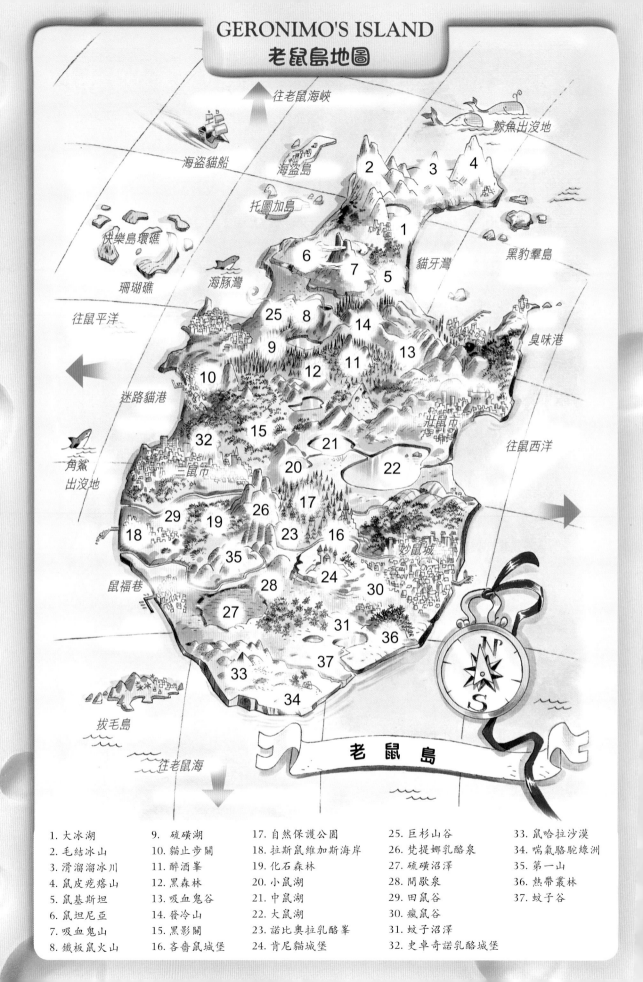

GERONIMO'S ISLAND
老鼠島地圖

往老鼠海峽

鯨魚出沒地

海盜貓船

海盜島

托圖加島

2
3
4

1

快樂島環礁

6

貓牙灣

黑豹羣島

珊瑚礁

海豚灣

7
5

往鼠平洋

25
8

14

臭味港

9

13

10

12
11

壯鼠市

往鼠西洋

迷路貓港

15

32

21

角鯊
出沒地

20

22

三鼠市

17

29
19
26

23
16

妙鼠城

18

35

24
30

鼠福巷

28

27

31
36

33

37

34

拔毛島

老 鼠 島

往老鼠海

Geronimo Stilton

EXERCISE BOOK
練習冊

想知道自己對 HOW OLD ARE YOU? 掌握了多少，
趕快打開後面的練習完成它吧！

ENGLISH!

4 HOW OLD ARE YOU? 你幾歲了？

HAPPY BIRTHDAY, BENJAMIN!
班哲文，生日快樂！

⭐ 請給班哲文的生日卡填上顏色，然後在橫線上給生日歌填寫完整。

Happy birth___ ___ ___ to you

___ appy birthday ___ ___ you!

Hap___ ___ ___ ___ ___ ___ ___ day,

dear ___ ___ ___ ___ ___ ___ ___ ___ !

Happy birthday to ___ ___ ___ !

MATCH AND COLOUR
配對和填色

⭐ 班哲文的生日派對快要開始了，看看他們準備了些什麼，把代表答案的英文字母寫在 ☐ 內。

A. table　　B. tablecloth　　C. napkin　　D. glass
E. plate　　F. fork　　G. spoon　　H. jug
I. ribbon　　J. balloons

FIND THE WORDS 尋字遊戲

⭐ 班哲文收到了什麼生日禮物？在下面的字母迷宮中找出生日禮物的英文名稱，並把它們圈起來。

book

basketball

poster

cap

cup

a	s	q	m	u	g	w	m	n	u	e
d	o	i	a	b	l	x	p	s	c	r
r	t	w	c	d	m	y	o	f	p	q
r	u	r	u	e	n	r	q	i	l	d
l	c	a	p	f	o	z	m	r	w	j
s	r	e	o	h	p	u	h	n	o	g
s	b	a	s	k	e	t	b	a	l	l
b	e	l	t	e	s	z	o	u	r	a
r	m	j	e	u	o	y	o	v	u	z
o	b	o	r	z	t	u	k	p	q	i
k	y	a	p	r	h	u	y	o	a	i

belt

3

LOOK AND FIND
觀察力大挑戰

⭐ 以下四幅圖看起來幾乎一樣，但事實上每個托盤上都有一種食物與其他托盤上的不同，請你把它圈起來，然後在橫線上寫出該食物的英文名稱。

提示：fruit cake   biscuits   sweets   apple

1.

_____

2.

_____

3.

_____

4.

_____

BIRTHDAY CAKE 生日蛋糕

★ 1. 你今年幾歲？請在蛋糕上畫出相應數量的蠟燭，然後給生日蛋糕填上顏色。

★ 2. 你今年幾歲？試用英語回答，並在橫線上寫上答案。

How old are you?

I am _____ .

WHAT DO YOU LIKE?
你喜歡吃什麼？

⭐ 請根據每個小朋友的話，在空框裏畫出他們喜歡的食物。如果他們說的是不喜歡的東西，可不要畫它啊！

1.
I like biscuits.

2.
I don't like sandwiches.

3.
I like sweets.

4.
I like ice cream.

I LIKE... I DON'T LIKE...
我喜歡…… 我不喜歡……

⭐ 在下面的橢圓形框內畫出兩種你不喜歡吃的食物，在長方形框內畫出兩種你喜歡吃的食物，然後在橫線上寫下每種食物的英文名稱。

I don't like...

I like...

_____

_____

_____

_____

ANSWERS 答案

TEST 小測驗

1. eleven, twelve, thirteen, fourteen, fifteen
2. ice cream, mini-pizzas, sweets, biscuits, orange juice, honey cake, lemonade
3. 略
4. present, book, T-shirt, basketball
5. (a) I like chocolate cake.   (b) I don't like cheese.   (c) I like sweets.   (d) I don't like mini-pizzas.

EXERCISE BOOK 練習冊

P.1

Happy birth<u>day</u> to you!

<u>H</u>appy birthday <u>to</u> you!

Happy <u>birth</u>day,

dear <u>Benjamin</u>!

Happy birthday to <u>you</u>!

P.2

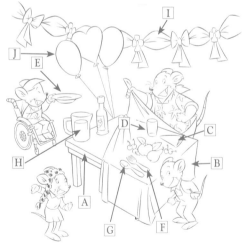

P.3

a	s	q	m	u	g	w	m	n	u	e
d	o	i	a	b	l	x	p	s	c	r
r	t	w	c	d	m	y	o	f	p	q
r	u	r	u	e	n	r	q	i	l	d
l	c	a	p	f	o	z	m	r	w	j
s	r	e	o	h	p	u	h	n	o	g
s	b	a	s	k	e	t	b	a	l	l
b	e	l	t	e	s	z	o	u	r	a
r	m	j	e	u	o	y	o	v	u	z
o	b	o	r	z	t	u	k	p	q	i
k	y	a	p	r	h	u	y	o	a	i

P.4

1. sweets   2. biscuits   3. fruit cake   4. apple

P.5-7

略